W9-ATY-668

TAKING TURNS

Herbster Readers

Written by Joanne Meier and Cecilia Minden • Illustrated by Bob Ostrom
Created by Herbie J. Thorpe

ABOUT THE AUTHORS

Joanne Meier, PhD, has worked as an elementary school teacher, university professor, and researcher. She earned her BA in early childhood education from the University of South Carolina, and her MEd and PhD in education from the University of Virginia. She currently works as a literacy consultant for schools and private organizations. Joanne lives in Virginia with her husband Eric, daughters Kella and Erin, two cats, and a gerbil.

Cecilia Minden, PhD, is the former director of the Language and Literacy Program at the Harvard Graduate School of Education. She is now a reading consultant for school and library publications. She earned her PhD in reading education from the University of Virginia. Cecilia and her husband, Dave Cupp, live outside Chapel Hill, North Carolina. They enjoy sharing their love of reading with their grandchildren, Chelsea and Qadir.

ABOUT THE ILLUSTRATOR

Bob Ostrom has been illustrating children's books for nearly twenty years. A graduate of the New England School of Art & Design at Suffolk University, Bob has worked for such companies as Disney, Nickelodeon, and Cartoon Network. He lives in North Carolina with his wife Melissa and three children, Will, Charlie, and Mae.

ABOUT THE SERIES CREATOR

Herbie J. Thorpe had long envisioned a beginning-readers' series about a fun, energetic bear with a big imagination. Herbie is a book lover and an avid supporter of libraries and the role they play in fostering the love of reading. He consults with librarians and matches them with the perfect books for their students and patrons. He lives in Louisiana with his wife Misty and their daughter Carson.

The Child's World

Published in the United States of America by The Child's World®
1980 Lookout Drive • Mankato, MN 56003-1705
800-599-READ • www.childsworld.com

Acknowledgments
The Child's World®: Mary Berendes, Publishing Director
The Design Lab: Kathleen Petelinsek, Design;
Gregory Lindholm, Page Production
Assistant colorist: Richard Carbajal

Library of Congress Cataloging-in-Publication Data
Meier, Joanne D.
  Taking turns / Joanne Meier and Cecilia Minden ; illustrated by Bob Ostrom.
    p. cm. — (Herbster readers)
  Summary: "A simple story belonging to the second level of Herbster Readers, young Herbie must learn to share and take turns when playing a board game."—Provided by publisher.
  ISBN 978-1-60253-014-0 (library bound : alk. paper)
  [1. Sharing—Fiction. 2. Bears—Fiction.] I. Minden, Cecilia. II. Ostrom, Bob, ill. III. Title. IV. Series.
  PZ7.M5148Tak 2008
  [E]—dc22   2008002593

It was a rainy day.

Herbie's dad heard loud voices.

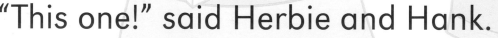

"This one!" said Herbie and Hank.

"No, this one!" said Hannah.

Herbie, Hannah, and Hank
were getting out some games.

They could not decide which one to play.

"Uh-oh," said Herbie's dad. "Looks like trouble."

"Playing a game should not make you fight!"

"Let's think about this," said Dad.

"Is there a better way
to choose a game?"

"We could take turns," said Hank.

"We could roll the dice to see who goes first," said Hannah.

"We could build a special machine to pick the winner!" said Herbie.

"Wow!" laughed Dad. "That would be great. But let's try the other ideas for now."

"Ok," said Herbie. "I have another idea."

29

"How about having fun?"

"That's the best idea yet," said Dad.